Billy *and the* Big New School

For Brodie

ORCHARD BOOKS
96 Leonard Street, London EC2A 4RH
Orchard Books Australia
14 Mars Road, Lane Cove, NSW 2066
ISBN hb 1 86039 207 5
ISBN pb 1 86039 524 4
First published in Great Britain in 1997
First paperback publication 1998
Text © Laurence Anholt 1997
Illustrations © Catherine Anholt 1997
The right of Laurence Anholt to be identified as the author of this work
and of Catherine Anholt as illustrator has been asserted by them in accordance
with the Copyright, Designs and Patents Act, 1988
A CIP catalogue record for this book is available from the British Library
Printed in Singapore

Billy *and the* Big New School

Pictures by Catherine Anholt
Story by Laurence Anholt

Billy was starting at a new school.

It was very exciting, but it made him feel a little funny inside.

On the Sunday before he started, Billy didn't feel like any breakfast at all. He kept thinking about that great big school and all the great big children.

Billy began to wish that he could stay at home with his mum.
"You're just like a little bird who doesn't want to leave his nest,"
said Billy's mum, giving him a hug.

Billy took the rest of his breakfast out to the bird table
and waited for the birds who were his friends. The birds weren't
scared of Billy because he was small like them and he knew how
to stand quite still.

Billy knew all the different birds. He had made pictures of them
for the kitchen walls. His mum had helped him write their names...

blackbird

starling

pigeon

thrush

sparrow

That Sunday morning Billy talked to the birds.
He told them about the new school.

He told them that he was worried in case he got lost…

or started to cry.

He told the birds that his mum had bought him new shoes with difficult laces.

"I wish I was a bird," said Billy. "Then I wouldn't have to worry about school at all. Or shoelaces."

Suddenly the birds started making a terrible noise.
Billy saw a new bird sitting on the ground. It was a tiny
sparrow. All the other birds were picking on it and
trying to chase it away.

But the little sparrow couldn't fly properly. It wasn't
really ready to look after itself.

It was the smallest, grubbiest, weediest, most dusty bird
Billy had ever seen. Billy called his mum.

Billy's mum ran out and chased the other birds away.
Then they carried the little sparrow inside.

The kitchen was warm, but the sparrow was shivering. Billy found the box from his new shoes.

He made a bed of cotton wool and put the bird gently inside. He could feel its little heart beating.

Then Billy gave the bird a bowl of water and a tiny piece of bread, but it wasn't hungry.

So Billy sat and talked gently to the sparrow.

All that Sunday the sparrow lay in the box and watched Billy with a big round eye.

And all that same Sunday Billy's mum got things ready
for the next day at the new school.

She wrote his name *Billy* on his clothes…   his bag…

his pencil case…   and the new shoes with the difficult laces.

That night, Billy had a scary dream. He dreamt that
he was a little bird who couldn't fly and the other birds
were picking on him.

Then his mum came in to the bedroom and gave
him a big hug. And Billy felt better.

In the morning, Billy woke up so early for school that it was still dark.

He had forgotten all about the little sparrow, until he walked into the kitchen and saw it sitting in the middle of the floor. It had hopped out of the shoe box all by itself.

"It must be feeling better," said Billy's mum. "I think it's time to let it go."

The bird had to go into the big world – just like Billy.

So Billy gently picked up the little bird and opened the window.

"You have to fly away," he whispered. "You have to learn to look after yourself like me."

The little bird looked up at Billy. It seemed to understand. Suddenly it hopped onto the windowsill and flew away into the sky.

After breakfast Billy took his new bag
and his mum helped him with his shoelaces.

Then it was time for school.

Billy's teacher was called Mrs Berry.
She was very nice.

She showed Billy where
to hang his coat...

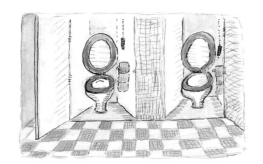

and where the
toilets were...

and the sink to
wash his hands...

and the paints...

and the computer...

and the playhouse...

and the reading corner.
Billy even found a big
book all about birds.

Some other children were new as well.

After a while, another boy came and looked at Billy's book too. Then Billy had a friend.

After lunch Mrs Berry talked to the class about animals. She asked if anyone had a pet.

Daisy had a dog.

Callum had a cat.

Jeremy had a gerbil.

Wendy had a worm.

Tom and Maddy, the twins, had a tortoise.
Billy was very interested.

"What about you, Billy?" asked Mrs Berry.

Billy thought for a moment. Then slowly he stood up.

In a tiny voice he began to tell everyone all about his bird table.
Then he told them about the poor little sparrow. And about how
he had put it in a shoe box until it was ready to fly...

When he had finished the story Mrs Berry began to clap.
And so did all the big children in Billy's class. Then Billy sat down.
His face was bright red. But his smile was the biggest in the school.

That night, Billy had another dream. But this one wasn't scary at all. He dreamt he could fly over the house, over the garden, over the town, and way over the big school, just like a bird. Billy and the birds flew high above the world and turned somersaults over the moon.

A few days later, Billy brought his new friend home from school.

They rolled about in the garden and got all dirty.
But Billy's mum didn't mind.

Billy and his friend had a picnic. They were very hungry.
All the birds came looking for crumbs.

Suddenly Billy saw one bird that looked almost exactly like the
sparrow from the shoe box. But he couldn't be quite sure because
this sparrow was bigger, and this sparrow was braver, and this sparrow
was happier, and this sparrow had lots of friends.

JUST LIKE BILLY.